FERGUSON
CAREER BIOGRAPHIES

TONY HAWK

Skateboarder and Businessman

Todd Peterson

Ferguson
An imprint of Facts On File

Tony Hawk: Skateboarder and Businessman

Ferguson
An imprint of Facts On File, Inc.
132 West 31st Street
New York NY 10001

ISBN-13: 978-0-8160-5893-8

Library of Congress Cataloging-in-Publication Data

Peterson, Todd (Todd D.), 1969-
Tony Hawk, skateboarder and businessman / Todd Peterson.
p. cm.
Includes bibliographical references and index.
ISBN 0-8160-5893-8 (hc : alk. paper)
1. Hawk, Tony. 2. Skateboarders—United States—Biography. 3. Businessman—United States—Biography. I. Title.
GV859. 813. H39A3 2005
796.22′092—dc22

2004008034

Ferguson books are available at special discounts when purchased in bulk quantities for businesses, associations, institutions, or sales promotions. Please call our Special Sales Department in New York at (212) 967-8800 or (800) 322-8755.

You can find Ferguson on the World Wide Web at http://www.fergpubco.com

Text design by David Strelecky

Pages 98–108 adapted from Ferguson's *Encyclopedia of Careers and Vocational Guidance, Twelfth Edition*

Printed and bound by Yurchak Printing, Inc., Landisville, Pa.
Printed in the United States of America

This book is printed on acid-free paper.

CONTENTS

1

THE 900

The last Sunday in June 1999, a chilly, overcast San Francisco day, represented the sort of gray year it had been for Tony Hawk. That year had not been one of Tony's best. The 31-year-old championship skateboarder was nearing the end of his career and had faced several difficult decisions. This particular day, however, would be one that Tony and his fans would never forget.

The X Games

ESPN's X Games—a competition for extreme sports such as skateboarding, surfing, and BMX bike riding—was wrapping up its fifth-year summer competition that Sunday in June. On Saturday, June 26, Tony had earned the bronze medal—his eighth X Games medal overall—when he finished a disappointing third on the vert ramp behind Bucky Lasek and Andy Macdonald. Vert, short for vertical, was the sort of ramp skateboarding style that Hawk had virtually defined during the past two decades.

Tony performs one of the airborne tricks that have made him famous. (Associated Press, CP)

Unlike street skating, which focuses on natural obstacles like concrete and railings and was the other type of skateboarding featured at the X Games, vert skating grew to be dominated by the ollie-style tricks popularized by Tony in the early 1980s.

The following day, during the best-tricks competition, Hawk skated with Lasek and Macdonald, as well as Colin McKay and Bob Burnquist, two other world-class champs. Halfway through the 30-minute competition, Tony landed a varial 720. This move had Hawk riding up one edge of the ramp backward, spinning two full rotations with his body while grasping his board, and finally turning the board 180 degrees so that he rode back down the ramp facing one side while his board faced the other. His moves were right on, but the rest of the skaters were pulling their best tricks, too.

The varial 720 was the trick Tony had counted on to win the contest, and with nearly 15 minutes left to compete and nothing else up his sleeve, he decided to try his luck with the 900.

The 900

The story of the 900 dated back 13 years. The 900 is a two-and-a-half revolution move for which a skater must gain the perfect height to rotate the necessary times and land upright on his or her board. Hawk had first imagined the trick in 1986 while teaching at a skating camp in France. While there, Tony had been practicing 540s—one-and-a-half revolutions—when he imagined adding another 360-degree rotation to the trick. Even though he conceived of the trick long ago, he had barely attempted the move since then.

As Tony explains in his autobiography, the 900—also known as a 9—required more than just tacking on an additional rotation to the 540: "We had learned 540s and then 720s, but the extra 180 degrees needed for the 9 was a nightmare. I felt I couldn't wind myself up that much and still maintain control. It wasn't a progression from the 720, but an entirely new trick." In order to pull a 9, the skater had to launch himself into the two-and-a-half spins and hit the board just right upon landing. There was only one option for not landing the trick: slamming into the ramp.

By the time the X Games rolled around in 1999, Tony had plenty of experience slamming. For two decades he had continuously devised new tricks and strived to perfect old ones. When they did not work—which was often—he crashed and burned. But the 900 was different. Failure to execute it meant more than scraped shins or bruised elbows. Falling meant a bone-rattling crash, a blow that could shake a skater to his very core. After 10 tries, says Hawk, it felt like walking away from a car crash.

In 1996 Tony began working on the "900 problem" religiously. But finding a good place to skate—never mind a place with the proper layout to pull off the stunt—was difficult. Skating was just starting to regain the popularity it lost in the late 1980s, when it was at its peak. Skate parks were not plentiful, even in southern California, the land of skating and surfing.

Tony started spending time riding with Danny Way and Colin McKay, both of whom skated for a company called Plan B. Their team had built a private indoor vert ramp in San Diego County. One day, while riding on Plan B's ramp, Tony felt good about trying a 900. He had been practicing the move for some time and had been having himself filmed while he tried it. Later, he would play back the film and dissect his attempts. This day he felt particularly good. The time felt right.

As he spun around and completed the trick, he briefly realized he was standing on his board—a success!—until he fell over and smacked the bottom of the ramp. He likened the feeling to skating into a wall. The result, he learned from his doctor, was a fractured rib.

After that Tony gave the 900 a rest for a while. Other skaters continued to edge closer to completing the trick, but no one could get it successfully. Tony became frustrated and tried the trick again, but also failed—with painful results.

By 1999 the 900 had become the stuff of legend. After landing the varial 720, Hawk thought he would try the trick in front of the thousands of skateboarding fans that had turned out that Sunday for the Games. As he tried one failed attempt at the 900 after another, Hawk zoned out. He knew he was not hitting his mark, but he felt incredibly close. The competition had wound to a close, the other skaters had left the ramp, but Hawk continued to skate.

As he repeatedly crashed to the ramp, he was vaguely aware of the announcer's voice informing him of his last try. But Tony was determined. He does not remember each successive slam into the flat bottom. Nor does he recall hiking back up to the top of the ramp to try the maneuver again. But after 11 failed attempts, on the 12th try, Tony Hawk realized that he was successfully rolling across the bottom of the ramp, upright. "All I could think was, '*Finally!*'" he wrote in his autobiography.

At the bottom of the ramp spectators and other skaters mobbed him. After 10 years of trying the 900, Hawk had successfully landed the impressive and dangerous stunt. Photographs of Tony after the fact show a jubilant, shouting athlete with his fist raised to the sky. Amid a crush of cameras, reporters, and well-wishers, Hawk proclaimed June 27, 1999, "the best day of my life."

2

EARLY YEARS

Tony Hawk, the youngest of four children, was born to Frank and Nancy Hawk on May 12, 1968, and by all accounts his entry into this world was a surprise to everyone. Tony's closest sibling, his brother Steve, was 12 years older than Tony. Besides Steve, Tony has two sisters, Patricia, who was 18 when Tony was born, and Lenore, who was 21 years old when Tony was born, both of whom were in college when Tony first came home from a San Diego hospital.

Tony thinks that it might have been this gap in age that explained the way his parents raised him. From the beginning Tony was an energetic and—according to some people—spoiled child. His parents, both nearing their mid-40s when he was born, were through raising children and had moved on to what Tony believes was more of a grandparenting phase. "Mom thought everything I did was cute, and I could do no wrong in my dad's eyes," says Tony.

Frank and Nancy's soft-handed approach to raising Tony was different from the way in which they had raised their other children. And Tony knew how to take advantage of their leniency. His parents, says Tony, were wrapped around his finger. And Tony himself was a bundle of energy—a self-described hyperactive kid.

Tony's ability to get away with any sort of behavior changed when he entered preschool. Being forced to follow school rules was a new and unpleasant situation for Tony. When Frank Hawk dropped him off at school, Tony would grip the chain-link fence and scream for his father. His behavior inside the school was not any better. Within a couple months the teachers had asked his parents to remove Tony from school, making him a certified preschool dropout. But his brief stay at school did show one thing about Tony: He was determined to get what he wanted at any cost. In the years to come, that determination would serve Tony the skater well.

Bad to the Bone

By the time he entered kindergarten, Tony had settled down a bit and had come to accept the inevitable: school. He was learning how to read and count, and soon he was working ahead of the other students. But his behavior at home was another matter. He was reaching a new high in lows. "I napalmed the house with my rampages. I was ridiculous," Tony later wrote.

Tony's outbursts were not limited to the home. In his autobiography, *Hawk: Occupation: Skateboarder*, Tony recalls many of the instances that made raising him a real challenge. In one such story, he relates his introduction to tennis, at the age of five. Nancy, his mother, thought Tony might like the game. Instead, Tony took the lesson as an excuse to try to nail his mother by aiming his shots directly at her. When she explained to him that the goal was not to hit your opponent with the ball, he was furious. In Tony's mind, if he could not destroy the competition, there was no use in playing. "What can I say? I was a hyper, rail-thin geek on a sugar buzz," he wrote.

When Tony was just starting school, there were hints of the type of person he would become. His parents were the first to see it. No matter how obnoxious or unruly Tony could be, there was one thing he refused to do: give up. No matter how hard anyone was on him, Tony was always harder on himself.

At the age of seven, Tony began to turn some of his energy toward sports. He joined Little League baseball and basketball and played both full tilt, even though he was not thrilled with the idea of team sports. Other players, thought Tony, just slowed him down. But Frank Hawk was proud of his son's participation, and soon Frank was coaching Tony's baseball team. Although Tony would continue playing both sports for the next few years, it was not until he was nine years old that he would be introduced to skateboarding. When Tony's brother Steve, who had since gone away to college, dug out the little fiberglass board he had skated on and gave it to Tony, Tony's initial reaction was to complain that he could not properly control it. Little did Tony realize how much direction he would give to and take from the sport of skateboarding.

Board Beginnings

At first Tony's used skateboard was just something else to pass the time and burn off some energy. Even after Steve had shown him some basic maneuvers, Tony picked up the board only on occasion. To the hyper young Tony, the four-wheeled board was just another thing, "like a Nerf football," he says. But years later he would realize that even then a seed had been planted in him.

It is fitting that Steve was the person who first introduced Tony to skateboarding. Steve was a surfer and an editor at *Surfer* magazine. The origins of skateboarding can be traced to the 1960s, when "sidewalk surfing" mimicked the motions of wave riders. Surfers had been cruising California's coastline for about three decades when the first skateboards were introduced. With boards that were little more than wood planks with metal wheels, many surfers took to the streets on these boards when the ocean lacked waves. Many of the moves these riders performed on their skateboards were intended to emulate the moves they did on their surfboards. But surfers were not the only people taking to the road. In the early 1960s, more than 50 million skateboards were sold. The sport literally exploded.

While surfers may have been free to do their thing out in the ocean, skateboarders proved to be a little too close to home for many pedestrians. In 1965 *Life* magazine ran an unfavorable story about the new sport. On the cover was a picture of a woman doing a handstand on a skateboard. Next to her, the title caption read, "The Craze and the Menace of Skateboards." Inside, the magazine lamented the "teeter-totter on wheels [that] is the new fad and menace." Although skateboarding was gaining in popularity, the sport was still very much in its infancy. Public outcry over the sport would cause it to disappear nearly altogether before Tony Hawk was even born.

By the time Tony first stepped onto his board, skateboarding already had a long and interesting history. Clay wheels had given way to urethane (a type of plastic) wheels, and the original wood boards were now made from fiberglass. But it was still just the beginning of a sport—one that Tony would see falter and nearly disappear a couple more times before becoming a bona fide form of competition.

The infamous 1965 Life *magazine cover photo; the magazine ran one of the first exposes on skateboarding.* (Time Life Pictures/Getty Images)

Tony on Wheels

By the time he was in the fourth grade, Tony was skating around the neighborhood with his friends. As his interest in skateboarding grew, Tony discovered Oasis Skatepark, the nearest skating facility, which was 15 minutes away from Tony's home near San Diego. Oasis consisted of a couple pools, a snake run, a half-pipe, a reservoir, and a beginner's section. Whenever Tony passed over the park, which was tucked under an Interstate overpass, he was mesmerized by the action of the skaters on the concrete below. As usual, Tony started in on his parents, demanding to be taken to the skate park. "Oasis wasn't the start of an intense infatuation with skateboarding," he writes in his autobiography. "It was just something that caught my attention and, naturally, I *had* to have it now—this instant."

Still, it was not until Tony was in fifth grade that his mom finally took him and a group of friends to Oasis. Frank had built Tony a small ramp in the family's driveway, but that had only kept Tony occupied for so long. By the time he finally reached Oasis, Tony had practically worked himself into a frenzy. Armed with his first real skateboard, a Sims model Frank had bought him, and outfitted with Oasis's smelly, sweat-soaked rental knee and elbow pads that were too big for him, Tony's first day skating at a real skate park gave him a sense of bliss. "It was a vacuum that sucked all my energy, and for the first time in my life I actually felt . . . content," says Tony. "It was an alien feeling."

That day marked a couple of huge turning points in Tony's life. For one, skating became his primary focus. His daily objective became scoring a ride to Oasis after school. The money that he earned from his paper route—Tony's first and only job other than skating—he used to finance his trips to the park. Yet there was another unexpected but welcome change in Tony's behavior. The self-centered, often bratty young kid had finally found an outlet to burn off some of the energy he frequently directed toward others. "When he started getting good at skating it changed his personality," says Tony's brother Steve. "Finally he was doing something that he was satisfied with. He became a different guy." Not only did Tony calm down; he started to think about how his actions affected other people. He became, says Steve, "more generous."

As he began to skate more and more, Tony's destiny became clearer to him. Although he was still playing baseball and basketball, Tony understood that he was driven to skate. Other sports did not interest him. "I just liked being freer, not having to submit to some practice schedule of repetitive passing and shooting, not having to rely on all the other players in order to do well," Tony later told a journalist. Finally he worked up the courage to tell his father that he wanted to quit playing baseball and basketball, which was a tough thing to admit since his father had been elected president of Little League. Frank Hawk took the news surprisingly well. He had always been supportive of his son, and Tony's love of skateboarding was no exception.

Up and Ollie

Tony's fascination with skating soon turned into a full-blown obsession. He would arrive early at school to skate before class started, and afterward he would head to Oasis, where he might stay until late into the evening. With the help of Dave Andrecht, one of the famous skaters of the late 1970s, Tony started practicing some of his first moves. These included rock 'n' rolls, in which you skate up to the edge of the ramp and hook your board on the lip, rotate your body 180 degrees, and skate back down, and rock to fakies, the same as a rock 'n' roll only without the 180-degree turn. It was also during this time that Tony learned the virtue of *airs*: skating while separated from the ground or ramp.

Tony had always been very thin; despite his high-sugar diet, his speedy metabolism burned off calories faster than he could pack them in. This presented a problem when it came to skating. In order to pull off the tricks that were popular at the time, skaters relied on a method called the "early grab," in which the rider grabbed the board out from under himself as he rode off the edge of the ramp. But this method required the skater to gain significant momentum, a force Tony could not achieve due to his thin frame. "I weighed slightly more than a Chihuahua," says Tony.

Instead, Tony used a new method to gain the air he needed to perform his tricks: He began to ollie. Although this technique would later become standard practice—and was the way in which Tony landed the 900 at the 1999 X Games—at the time ollieing was regarded as an inferior style.

An ollie, so named for the 13-year-old skateboarder Alan "Ollie" Gelfand who invented it, consists of popping your board up with your back foot while stabilizing it with your front foot so you and your board become airborne. Gelfand had created the trick in 1976 in order to cope with poor skating conditions in his hometown of Hollywood, Florida.

By the time Gelfand retired from skating in 1981, skateboarding wasn't very popular, and neither was the ollie. Fortunately, Tony Hawk never cared about what other people thought was a fad. Tony did ollies out of necessity, because of his lack of upper-body strength. But for many other skaters, ollieing was considered "cheating"—even if it was not any easier to perform. As a result of their strength, other skaters could simply swing their boards around in the air.

Tony faced a lot of criticism during his early career for ollieing. But by 1999, the method Tony began to use out of necessity had become the way in which nearly every vert skater at X Games V executed his moves.

A Fast Ride

Tony began improving on the board with lightning speed. While part of his success as a skateboarder is his natural inclination to the sport, many of Tony's accomplishments can be attributed to his relentless work. Skating helped tame the hyper young athlete, perhaps because Tony focused every last bit of his energy into it.

At Oasis, he relied on the help of older skaters such as Andrecht to improve his own style. Despite Tony's calmer demeanor, some aspects of his behavior did not change. For instance, whenever he saw a more experienced skater perform a trick he liked, Tony would often try to make the trick his own, performing it over and over again. "I could be the biggest idiot without realizing it," he later wrote. "I'd watch people skate and say, 'Wow! Did you see that trick that he did? I'd better try that!' Then I'd attempt it in front of the person who'd just done it." It was not until he was much older, says Tony, that he realized just what an insult that sort of behavior can be.

His family also had to deal with Tony's insistence on being the best. On more than one occasion, Tony kept his father waiting in the car at Oasis while he attempted to learn a new trick, such as the time he spent an entire day practicing frontside rock 'n' rolls. When Frank came to drag him home, Tony complained that he needed only 500 additional tries to perfect the move—and he was serious.

Tony's dedication to skating finally started to pay off when he was 11. That year he entered his first competition, held at Oasis Skatepark. Although Tony had logged many hours skating its ramps, he did horribly in the event. "I was so nervous that I fell on tricks I could normally do blindfolded," he says. But his first contest did not discourage him. Instead, he began to seek out new skate parks, and he continued riding as much as ever.

Soon Tony was entering contests up and down the southern California coast. His preparation for these competitions was filled with the same zeal with which Tony approached everything. He would spend hours skating the park where upcoming competitions were to be held. He would methodically diagram on paper every trick he intended to perform and at which part of the park he would perform it. And he would usually end his run with a trick—the first in a long line of many—that he had created: the backside varial, which is done while the skater rides up the wall and grabs his board from behind and between his legs and rotates it while jumping.

Some contests went better than others. But for the first year he competed, Tony still could not shake the queasy

In the early 1980s, when Tony was just beginning to skate, skateboarding was considered an activity for outcasts. Most people did not recognize it as a sport. (Associated Press)

nervousness he felt before each competition. Now a student at Jean Farb Middle School in San Diego, Tony was undeniably hooked on skating. And soon skating would be hooked on him. After a year of competing, Tony was awarded a spot on Oasis's skate park team.

Who Skates?

In 2000, one of Tony's old teachers would ask the now world-famous skater to return to Farb Middle School to participate in a reading group for students. Despite efforts to make Tony's visit a low-key affair, word spread throughout the school that the famous skater was on the premises. Students mobbed the hallway outside the classroom and another adult reading-group participant, a police officer, escorted Tony from the school in his cruiser. Of the event, Tony would later write, "Eighteen years ago I was considered an outcast and a nerd in this neighborhood because I skated, and now I needed a police escort to leave it safely."

In the early 1980s skateboarding was an activity of outcasts. Despite the contests, events, and skating's popularity in the 1960s and '70s, skateboarding was not even really considered a sport by most people. The X Games were nearly 15 years away, and skating, which had been on a steady decline since its peak 10 or 15 years earlier, was losing fans. None of this had any effect on Tony. He continued to skate as much as ever, but he found fewer people to skate with. One by one the skate parks Tony had visited across southern California were closing their doors. But Oasis remained open. During a contest at the park, Tony won his first sponsorship from Dogtown, a skateboard manufacturer.

During this period, Frank Hawk helped organize the California Amateur Skateboard League (CASL). But despite the enthusiasm for skateboarding in the Hawk household, most Americans were not interested. Tony's time away from school was spent either at Oasis or at contests at the few parks that had remained open. While he was in school, he was regarded as somewhat of an oddity. "I looked like a B-movie mummy . . ." says Tony. "Scabs ran the entire length of my legs, and my sprained wrists and elbows were wrapped tight with Ace bandages. At the skate park this was considered normal, but at school it was a different matter."

How other people viewed him did not matter much to Tony. In 1980 he was 12 years old, barely four feet tall, and weighed about 80 pounds. But Tony's smallness had not stopped some of the biggest names in skateboarding from noticing him. That same year Stacy Peralta, the retired world-champion skater of the 1970s, asked Tony to join his Powell Peralta team (the company was named for cofounder George Powell).

Powell Peralta, commonly known as Powell, was one of many equipment manufacturers of the time that also sponsored its own team. G&S, another major company, also asked Tony to join its team. Dogtown, Tony's first sponsor, had gone out of business, and both Powell and G&S hoped to lure him. Finally, Tony decided to join the Powell team, which was known as the Bones Brigade. He would spend the next 13 years of his life skating with the team.

3

LEARNING TO BE A PRO

Tony's ascension to the Bones Brigade did not mark an immediate improvement in either his skating or his life off the board. By the time Tony had entered the eighth grade, he was forced to transfer to nearby Serra High School, which included classes for eighth and ninth graders. Still incredibly small for his age and with clothes that were shredded from skating and emblazoned with logos, Tony became the target of some kids. Try as he might to blend in, his size and clothes too often gave him away. And no one who was anyone would be caught dead skating.

That did not stop Tony. In the early 1980s he had started to spend most of his time skating at Del Mar Surf and Turf, a skate park five minutes away from his parents' new home in Cardiff, California. It was there that Tony was photographed for his first cover of *Thrasher*, then a new skateboarding magazine out of San Francisco. Del

Mar would become Tony's home skate park for years to come.

Lots to Learn

Tony still had plenty of things to learn on the board. When he joined the Powell team at 12 years old, Tony began competing in national events. His first out-of-town competition with the Bones Brigade was in Jacksonville, Florida, and despite the team's positive finish overall, Tony's performance was forgettable. "I couldn't have skated more terribly if I'd tried," he writes in his autobiography.

Despite his poor showing in Florida, Tony continued to improve. Skateboarding still was unpopular, but die-hard skaters continued to show up for events and competitions. Tony became aware of just how good other skaters were—and just how much work he had to do in order to become the skater that he wanted to be.

In 1982 Tony turned 14. Shortly thereafter he turned "professional." Tony was preparing to compete at a contest in Whittier, California, when Stacy Peralta sidled up next to Tony as he was registering and asked if he was going to turn pro. Tony, who had not given the matter much thought, said "Sure."

Unlike today, in 1982 being a pro skater did not mean much. There were only a handful of pros, and skating was not a way to make a living (not that Tony needed to; he was only 14). Top prize money at a contest might be $150, if that. When Tony broke the news of his professional status to his parents, they said, "That's nice."

In ninth grade Tony's parents relocated to a nearby neighborhood and he was moved to another high school, San Dieguito. This school taught grades nine through 12, so Tony was back at the bottom of the pack as he had been at Serra. And despite his status as a professional skateboarder, the students at San Dieguito were not any friendlier. Tony still looked very young, and skateboarding had not yet come back into fashion. Plus, his hair and clothes—bleach-blond bangs and skater shorts—were light years ahead of early 1980s fashion. "I wore weird clothes, was obsessed with a 'loser' sport, and looked like I'd got lost on my way to elementary school," Tony writes.

But his move to pro status was not entirely without its rewards. At his second contest as a pro, Tony won first place, beating old-school skater Duane Peters. This victory laid the foundation for a new type of skating with more innovative moves on the board. Tony Hawk was getting ready to change the face of skating forever.

Old Versus New

Before the ollie, the old style of skateboarding had relied on power tricks such as carving, which is riding low and close to the ground, and early grabs. But Tony did not have much choice as to how he skated. He still had to ollie in order to gain the air necessary to perform tricks.

A few other professional skaters claimed that Tony "skated like a geek." His style was definitely a new way of skating. He was creating tricks like the fingerflip backside air, in which he grabbed the nose of the board and spun it in a full 180-degree rotation. Other skaters, says Tony, thought of the move as a joke. Among some of the pros Tony became known as the "Circus Skater." But he was not kidding around.

Today, after more than two decades of competitive skating, Tony is responsible for the creation of more than 80 tricks. Although more skaters are drawn to street skating these days, vert skaters like Tony continue to inspire and impress skateboarders of all types. Some of the maneuvers Tony devised are so complex and performed at such lightning speed that even seasoned skaters may have trouble immediately identifying them. There are a select few of Tony's tricks, in fact, that he had abandoned due to their difficulty.

But when he was first starting out, Tony had no idea the sort of influence he would eventually wield on skateboarding. Despite poor showings in the next couple competitions following his first-place win, Tony did not get discouraged. He was still hard on himself, locking himself in

Tony tackles the half-pipe during vert practice, 2002. (Landov)

his bedroom and staring off into space when he finished badly. While he spent all his free time at Del Mar, Tony continued to struggle with his status as an outsider at school. But he never let that get in the way of his schoolwork. Although skating was never far from his thoughts, Tony was in some advanced classes and pulling down a B average. Professional skateboarding was not a career option at that time. "Back then nobody made a decent living from skateboarding, so I never counted on it as a career," says Tony. Instead, he planned on going to college to study physics.

Mom, Dad, and the NSA

Looking back on his upbringing, Tony says, "We weren't your stereotypical family." For one thing, there was the age separating Tony and his siblings. Also, Frank and Nancy Hawk were older than most parents who had children Tony's age, but they took chances many other adults would not have. Nancy, for example, had returned to school at age 38. While working full time, she took night classes, and eventually earned her master's degree when she was in her 50s and a Ph.D. in education when she was 62. Frank had been a decorated Navy pilot in World War II and the Korean War before returning home to become a salesman. Both parents were extremely devoted to their children's interests.

Thus, in 1983, Frank started the National Skateboard Association (NSA). In the absence of any other such organization to govern skateboard contests, Frank wanted to bring structure to the sport Tony loved. Skateboarding companies approved the idea, and the NSA was soon up and running.

Although the NSA added much needed structure to competitive skating, its formation actually hurt Tony at first. The first national contest sponsored by the NSA was held at Del Mar. It was no secret that Tony skated better at Del Mar than anywhere else. Even though Frank had no involvement with the judging of contests, people were suspicious because the contest was run by the organization that Frank founded and was being held on Tony's home turf. But other skaters soon came around and began to realize just how devoted Tony's parents were to the sport.

During this time, Tony was coming into his own as a professional. The division between freestyle skating (which would later become street skating) and vert skating (on ramps, pools, and half-pipes) increased. Even among vert skaters, the types of tricks they performed were becoming more sophisticated. Riding hard, grinding the board, and carving moves like surfers do were becoming things of the past. The tricks many vert skaters were pulling were starting to look a lot like the "circus" tricks Tony did. That other vert skaters were learning from Tony was only one of the many evolutions skating underwent. For his part, Tony acknowledges a debt to such freestylers as Rodney Mullen and Per Welinder, who he says influenced his "flippy, freestyle tricks."

Tony spent the summer of 1983 doing skating demonstrations, or demos, in Europe, Australia, and the United States. Skate demos are exhibitions usually put on by parks or shops so pro skaters can demonstrate their abilities. That same year, Stacy Peralta asked Tony for a logo that would be used on the first Tony Hawk skateboard for Powell Peralta. Skaters on teams made money from royalties of boards sold with their designs. Tony submitted a sketchy line drawing of a swooping hawk, which he intended to use only as the basis for his first design. Stacy went ahead and passed on the drawing as the final design. Soon, Tony's first board was in production. He was paid 85 cents per board sold. His first royalty check: 85 cents.

A Video Star

Despite the fact that Tony's next royalty check was $4.25, Powell discontinued the board in favor of a new design, a screaming hawk skull with a beak or, the name Tony preferred, the Screaming Chicken Skull. The graphic, a classic logo still recognized today, would prove to be Tony's best-selling board design ever.

Tony started to rip it up elsewhere. He won a competition in St. Petersburg, Florida. It was the first contest he had won outside of his home park at Del Mar. But little had changed at school. He was still attending San Dieguito, where he was at the mercy of kids who had no idea what a skateboard even was. When he went out into the skating world, however, Tony was signing autographs and selling boards with his logo on it. The Screaming Chicken Skull proved to be an instant hit, and soon Tony was pulling in $500–$1,000 per month in royalty fees. It was, says Tony, "serious cash to a 15-year-old in 1983."

Tony also became an unexpected video star, thanks to Stacy Peralta's Bones Brigade videos. Part miniature action-films and part documentaries, these videos were shot when VCRs were just beginning to make their way into American homes. They were funny, irreverent, and captured incredible skating on tape—so much so that the *Bones Brigade Video Show* continues to influence skaters today. The tapes were a hit. Sales of Hawk's board began to generate $3,000 a month for the young skater.

By the time Tony was ready to enter the 10th grade in the fall, he decided that he had had enough of San Dieguito High School. Tony switched schools to nearby Torrey Pines, whose students were more interested in surfing than in hassling skateboarders. And then slowly, skateboarding began to regain some of its former popularity. At the same time, skater Mike McGill invented the 540 McTwist, a trick that would further divide the vert-skating world and send all riders—Tony included—scrambling to learn it.

Spinning On to Better Things

McGill had devised the 540 McTwist while teaching a summer skate camp in Sweden. Mike tried to keep the trick a secret, but when he returned to California he used it in a contest at Del Mar. The 540 is a one-and-a-half rotation turn in the air. With the McTwist, the skater tucks his head so that he rotates and turns upside down in a sort of corkscrew motion. In order to make the entire motion, the rider must really ratchet up his or her body so that it rotates and twists correctly.

Tony would later say that the 540 became his favorite move, but back then it took him more than two months to finally execute one. But he was not the only skater vexed by the fancy-looking maneuver. "It was the first time I can remember vert pros all concentrating on learning one trick," Tony says. Soon it became *the* trick to pull off in contest runs, and the skaters who could not do it rarely won.

World Champion

Skating is not a sport like football or basketball, in which it is easy to determine the winner. Skaters are awarded points for the tricks they perform during their runs. Judges watching skaters award points based on how they feel about the tricks being performed. One judge may rate a certain style very different from another judge's rating. "Skating is not like gymnastics or figure skating, with predetermined points for tricks," Tony writes in his autobiography. "*How* you do a trick can be just as important as the trick itself."

In the NSA, skaters were awarded points based on how they finished in contests. Although 1983, Tony's first year as a pro, had been kind of spotty—he had placed first, fourth, sixth, and 15th in various contests—he had accumulated enough points to become the National Skateboard Association's first world champion. The award did not mean much to Tony. He had always been more interested in competing against himself than in being measured against other skaters. But the NSA award proved significant because it would be the first of many. Tony's pro career was about to take off.

Something continued to bug the young skater, however. Despite his first-place NSA finish, Tony still lacked confidence in his skating ability. This was not helped by comments from other pros, some of whom claimed that Tony's style was robotic. Even with everything that had been changing in the world of skating, Tony Hawk was still very much an outsider.

Soon enough, though, Tony would have little choice but to accept how he skated. He was entering his junior year of high school at Torrey Pines, and the demands on his time were becoming greater and greater. Many weekends were taken up with traveling and demos as skating continued to regain its popularity. It was during one of these weekend trips that he first met Cindy Dunbar, whom he would one day marry. He finished the 1984 skate season strongly, finishing in one of the top three spots for every contest he entered over the year. Those showings earned Tony another NSA world-champion award.

To his relief, Tony had grown quite a bit. Although still quite thin, he was now six feet tall, and his larger frame helped him to improve his skating. He started 1985 by winning his first three professional contests, the first pro skateboarder ever to do so. That summer he traveled to Sweden to teach a five-week skating camp with Lance Mountain and Rodney Mullen. While there, Tony landed his first 720—two full rotations in the air. The trick was fairly easy to learn, Tony says, but whenever he landed it, he ended up squatting on the board. It took him several years to complete a 720 in the upright position.

Video Sequel

Stacy Peralta's *Bones Brigade Video Show* had hit big with skateboarders in 1983. Two years later Peralta began work on the second Bones Brigade video, *Future Primitive*. This video was a step up from the team's first one, and it played well as skating increased in popularity. Tony started to receive fan mail, and Powell Peralta skateboards continued to sell better than ever. Tony was 17 years old, and he was earning $7,000 a month in royalties.

At the same time, Tony was perfecting many of his signature tricks such as the Airwalk, which later inspired the shoe and clothing company of the same name. Moves like Saran Wrap, a trick so named for Nancy Hawk's fondness of leftover food, required Tony to wrap his foot around the board while in the air. The Stalefish, inadvertently named when a skater misread some of Tony's handwritten notes, consisted of grabbing the board from behind between your legs. All the moves were unique, unusual, and every bit Tony Hawk.

In the fall of 1985 Tony started his senior year. As his schedule got busier, he had less time to devote to school. This had been true throughout much of Tony's school life, yet he had always found a way to maintain decent grades. That became more challenging in his final year, as Tony struggled to balance his skateboarding career with school. By the time the first semester was over, Tony had again won the NSA's world-champion award—for the third time.

All of Tony's hard work was beginning to pay off. He was earning so much money that, during his senior year, his sister Patricia advised him to buy a house in order to invest some of it. Other people were beginning to notice

Once Tony finished high school, skateboarding became his full-time career. (Landov)

him, too. When Tony appeared in a television ad for a soda brand, many of his classmates saw him on TV. All of a sudden the same people who had either bullied or shunned him throughout school were interested in this famous skater. But by then high school was nearly over. Shortly before graduation Tony moved into his new house, only a few minutes away from his parents' house. And when school was finished, Tony embarked on his full-time skateboarding career.

Working at Skating

Following graduation Tony went on tour with the Bones Brigade. During these road trips Tony and the rest of the team put on demos at parks across the country. For Tony, the trips were a lot of fun: A bunch of young skaters piled into a van, visited parks all over the United States, and were paid to skate.

Not long after this tour Tony scored his first bit part in a Hollywood movie. He was cast as an extra in the film *Thrashin',* the story of two rival skateboard gangs battling one another for supremacy. The film featured many hot skaters besides Tony, including Steve Caballero, Tony Alva, Christian Hosoi, and others. But Tony was mostly interested in his part because he was allowed to skate at Del Mar where the filming was taking place. The park, Tony's home base for many years, had recently closed for good.

Of course, by this time Tony was no stranger to the camera. The Bones Brigade crew quickly started work on *The Search for Animal Chin*, Stacy Peralta's third video of the Powell team. The filming of *Animal Chin* took four months. It was Peralta's and the team's most inspired video and featured some of the best skating ever caught on tape. Between the tour and *Chin*, Tony continued to skate in contests, racking up six first-place finishes in 1986. It was enough to earn him another—his fourth—NSA world championship.

Without a doubt, Tony had worked hard to help revive skateboarding. Although he still was criticized for his unusual style, many young skating fans loved the way he rode. When skateboarding fully rebounded in 1987, Tony was in a great place. He skated with the hottest team in the world, had appeared in the Bones Brigade videos, sold boards with his graphic at a staggering rate, and may have been the most recognized skater anywhere. But with these great successes came burdens that were starting to take their toll on the 19-year-old Tony.

Out of the Game

Twelve years later, after successfully completing his first 900, Tony would say, "Skating is not about winning, it's about skating the best you can and mutual appreciation.

It's about pulling a trick after years of not being able to and having other skaters be happy for you." That was the attitude Tony had always held toward skating. The only person he was ever interested in competing against was himself. Since he had started winning one contest after another several years earlier, other skaters began to hold him up to incredibly high standards. "In a lot of people's eyes, if I didn't win an event, then I simply lost," says Tony. It was not the way he wanted to skate.

Now contests were drawing thousands and thousands of people, and Tony continued grabbing first- and second-place wins. He was making more money than ever, not just from his Powell board sales but also from other sponsors that paid him to wear their clothing or endorse their equipment. Amid all this, at age 19 Tony decided to retire from professional skateboarding.

It was not a spur-of-the-moment decision. Tony wrestled with his options. He invited his brother Steve over to his house to help him work out his problems. Almost since the day he had turned professional, the pressure had been building around Tony. His climb to the top of the skating world was so swift and so decisive that other skaters began to tell him they just hoped to finish in second place when they competed against him, realizing that the number-one spot almost always went to Tony.

If Tony did not win a contest in which he was entered, it was as if he had failed. Those types of demands began to become too much for the young Tony to handle.

Together, he and Steve decided that retiring might be Tony's best choice. Now Tony had to break the news to Bones Brigade team leader Stacy Peralta.

Steve drove Tony to Stacy's house, and on the way there Tony hardly said a word. The situation did not improve when they arrived. Years later Tony would remember the scene as a bit overdramatic, but at the time it was the most difficult decision he had ever had to make. Stacy had no idea why Tony was there. In fact, neither Stacy—nor anyone else close to Tony—had any idea that he was suffering under these pressures. It was typical of Tony's nature to keep his problems to himself until they became so large they had to be dealt with.

To Tony's surprise, Stacy completely supported his decision. Stacy had also retired at about the same age, and he wanted Tony to do what was right for himself. But at that time, Stacy also understood Tony even better than Tony understood himself. Stacy saw in Tony his desire to compete, and there was little doubt in his mind that Tony would return to competition.

In the years that followed, Tony would come to understand exactly what Stacy had done to support him. From the beginning Stacy had been aware of Tony's unique style and the negative image it created among other skaters. But instead of downplaying it, Stacy helped to highlight and popularize Tony's way of skating. Tony later joked, "My entire career would have been different if Stacy hadn't had the confidence in my skating to pull us both through the rough times."

Despite what Stacy might have known about Tony, when Tony broke the news to him in 1987, Stacy still stood to lose a great deal from Tony's retirement. Tony's board was Powell Peralta's hottest item, and every skating magazine in the country was slapping Tony all over its pages. But Stacy stood by Tony, and even wrote him a letter of encouragement after their meeting. Tony Hawk was officially retired.

Away from the Board

Tony's retirement may have been one of skating's shortest. He continued to practice, but he avoided competition for three months. In that time a number of changes took place in Tony's life. The biggest was the beginning of his relationship with Cindy Dunbar.

Although the two had known one another for several years, they had just maintained a long-distance friendship. Cindy lived in Fresno, California, more than 300 miles north of Tony's home in Carlsbad. But over time their relationship became more serious, and finally Tony asked her to move in with him. At the same time Tony had his eye on a new house, which was located on a four-acre lot several acres away from the nearest neighbor.

Soon, Tony had his second house and crew of skaters, plus his dad, Frank, putting together a complicated series of ramps. It had taken more than a month to design the seven-foot mini ramp, the 40-foot-wide main ramp, and the seven-foot-deep bowl. The new house was located in Fallbrook, California. The small town, isolated in the southern California desert, seemed to be an ideal spot to throw up a ramp. Despite Tony's intention to retire from skating, he could not stop competing.

In early 1988 Tony and Cindy moved into the new house in Fallbrook. After his brief break from competition, Tony started to enter contests again. He felt a new sort of self-assurance since he had expressed his concerns to Stacy. That confidence showed in his riding, and soon he was in top form. Skating contests and demos continued to draw thousands of fans, and it was not unusual for Tony and the other members of the Bones Brigade to spend hours signing autographs.

As the summer heated up, Tony was busier than ever. He spent nearly three months on tour in the United States, Europe, Australia, and New Zealand. That fall Tony appeared in his fourth Bones Brigade video, *Public Domain*. The year that had begun with Tony's retirement had ended up to be his most financially successful yet. His career had been supercharged by the much-needed break, but little did Tony know that skateboarding was about to undergo a complete upheaval.

4

THE LEAN YEARS

Even as skateboarding was regaining its popularity through the late 1980s, skating styles were changing in ways that would alter the sport forever. Although 1989 was a banner year for four wheeling, Tony remembers it as the year in which skating actually split in half. In the same way that freestyle skating had given way to vert skating nearly a decade earlier, a new type of skating was gaining in popularity.

Street skating—"street," for short—grew out of the many skaters who either did not want or could not afford to skate at parks or on ramps. Street combined some of the tricks vert skaters used along with an array of new and old freestyle tricks. The emphasis was on skating natural surfaces: sidewalks, benches, curbs, and the like. Most of the vert skaters that Tony knew also did a little bit of street skating, but most of them were not very serious about it.

But slowly, a younger generation of skaters began taking to their boards—and most of them were riding in the streets. By 1989 street skating had surpassed vert skating in popularity.

Tony never devoted too much time to street skating. For one thing, the chances of getting injured were generally greater on the street. Street skaters have a tendency to push it a little harder and to take much greater risks than vert skaters. Even today, many skaters view street skating as a "purer" form of the sport. For Tony, these risks were hard on his vert-skating body. He was used to being scrapped and banged-up, but street skating presented other, more dangerous, obstacles, such as the time Tony slammed into a marble bench with his shin. The collision left a 2-inch hole in Tony's leg.

With the growing popularity of street skating came a major overhaul to the skateboarding industry. Companies like Powell, Sims, Santa Cruz, and others had once dominated the skating world with their equipment and high-profile skaters. Powell Peralta, in particular, was the brand to have. But as street skating grew, that was quickly changing. A number of newer and smaller companies were springing up, selling their own equipment and sponsoring their own skaters. They were cutting into big companies like Powell and taking their business away, and skaters such as Tony were feeling the pinch.

Vert versus Vert

At the same time that street was asserting itself, another revolution in skating was under way. By the late 1980s, a number of new vert skaters such as Colin McKay and Danny Way were gaining in popularity. Skate fans were on the lookout for fresh faces and rising talent. As these young skaters came on the scene, they were inevitably compared with their older counterparts such as Tony. A lot of people wanted to see the young new skaters replace the "dinosaurs" like Tony, who had recently turned 21 years old.

These were not the only changes bothering Tony. In a few short years skating had exploded. The sport was larger than life, and with its popularity came new attitudes toward skating. No longer was it just about riding hard and having a good time with your friends. Skating now had an image. "Being a skater wasn't enough anymore," Tony later wrote. "You had to be a cool skater."

Regardless of how Tony felt about these two new challenges, he knew fresh vert skaters and street skating were here to stay. But there was a price to be paid. Powell Peralta's era was coming to an end, and the Bones Brigade was slowly crumbling with it. Tony and many others consider *Ban This*, the sixth video in the Bones Brigade series, to have been the beginning of the end for Powell.

Shot on Tony's ramps at his Fallbrook house, *Ban This* features amazingly good vert skating as all the Bones

Brigade videos had. But it was lacking in the sort of raw, dangerous footage that the smaller street-skating companies were releasing. Change was in the air.

Injury and Recovery

Tony, meanwhile, had other problems to deal with. While attempting a 720 at a demo in Japan, Tony felt his knee pop. He was no stranger to various pops, scrapes, or other minor injuries, and he was not concerned with this one. But later that day he bent over and his knee locked in the bent position. He knew something was wrong. Tony returned home and went to a doctor who discovered that Tony had torn the cartilage in his knee. That same cartilage was getting jammed under his kneecap, and was causing his knee to lock in odd positions.

In order to fix it, Tony would require knee surgery. After more than 10 years of skateboarding—six of them as a professional—Tony was facing his first serious injury on the board. Despite his upcoming surgery, Tony still entered a contest in Hawaii. It was the last National Skateboarding Association competition that Frank Hawk would be involved with: Tony's father was preparing to retire from his NSA role.

Tony had surgery when he returned home, and his recovery kept him off his skateboard for four months. But there was no question as to Tony's strength when he climbed back on his board. He ended 1989 with eight more contests, five of them first-place finishes, and another NSA championship.

Tony also appeared in a bit role in the film *Gleaming the Cube*. The film's title, which was a nonsensical gag that had accidentally been lifted from an interview in a skateboarding magazine, was a running joke among skaters. But the movie, about a skater who tries to get revenge on the men who killed his brother, afforded Tony the opportunity to actually act a little bit in his character of a pizza delivery guy.

Like all skateboarders, Tony has had his share of injuries. Moments like these could end disastrously if the skater loses concentration or is not wearing protective gear. (Getty Images)

The year proved to be Tony's most successful yet, but his time with Powell Peralta and the Bones Brigade was coming to an end.

A Downhill Slide

By the time he was 21 years old Tony was the most successful skater in board history. His unorthodox style had earned him a legion of fans, and his gutsy moves had placed him at the top of the skating heap for more than five years. But his rise to the top had not always been easy. When Tony had begun competing as an amateur in the early 1980s, skateboarding was dead. At that time skaters had abandoned the sport, just as they had 10 years earlier at the start of the 1970s. It was a cycle that seemed to repeat itself every decade. And by the beginning of the 1990s, many people in the industry saw another skating drought coming on.

Despite street skating's newfound success and the battles of new versus old on the vert ramps, in 1990 people began to drop out of skating at an alarming rate. What had been the hottest thing around a year earlier dried up overnight. For Tony, it was as if the world had suddenly looked at what he was doing and declared it "all wrong." To make matters worse, skating's demise caught him off guard. While skating had been going strong, Tony had spent money freely. During the last few years of the 1980s Tony had earned considerably more than $100,000 a year.

But he had spent much of it as quickly as he earned it. After all, he had two houses: his Fallbrook home and the first house he purchased in Carlsbad, California. He also had a serious affection for gadgets, and he pumped a lot of his money into all the newest electronic toys. Besides that, Tony was generous with his money. He bought airplane tickets for his friends so that they could travel with him, and he spent plenty at restaurants. He was used to living as he pleased. And then, even quicker than he had started to earn them, his royalty checks dried up. At first they were slightly smaller than they had been; then they were half of what they had been. Before long, he was earning a small fraction of what he earned just a year earlier. Suddenly, his opulent lifestyle was ending.

The money from skateboarding was gone because the fans were gone. Contests that had drawn thousands of fans just a few months before could not turn out even a hundred now. "I did demos where I could count the spectators on two hands," Tony told one reporter. Aside from a group of hard-core professional skaters, most followers of the sport had turned their attention to other things.

Life Changes

During this period Tony's personal life took a serious turn as well. In 1990 Tony married Cindy Dunbar, who had been living with him at the Fallbrook house since 1988.

The couple was married in the backyard of their home. Half of the guests were told the wrong time and showed up after the ceremony, and the justice of the peace hired to marry them addressed Tony by the wrong name. The wedding, as Tony remembers it, was a little bit "different."

Meanwhile, skating's freefall continued. Tony's boom career had officially gone bust, and Cindy, a manicurist, started to earn more money doing nails than Tony earned from skating. Tony rented out his house in Carlsbad, and Cindy gave him a food allowance that he used as "Taco Bell money."

Although the downward trend in skating continued, Tony did not stop competing. In 1991 he entered nine contests, finishing in first place in seven of them. At the same time, Tony's dissatisfaction with Powell Peralta increased. The once-small board manufacturer had grown into a huge company. Powell had become too big and too slow to react to the changes in the sport as vert skating continued plummeting. Never one to shy away from risk, Tony wanted to promote his future in skating—whatever might be left of it—on his own terms. Together with Swedish skater Per Welinder, Tony started his first company, Birdhouse Projects. The name was taken from a nickname Tony got because of his high-flying aerial stunts: the Birdman.

Birdhouse was a huge gamble from the start. To get the company up and running, Tony had to borrow money against his house in Carlsbad—a move that could have meant losing the home if Birdhouse failed. But, as Tony figured, his professional career was drawing to a close. He was almost 24 years old, and he thought he had maybe another couple years of skating at best. With skateboarding in the tank, he felt that he had to take control of his future.

Per had also skated with Powell, and Tony knew him quite well. He had some of the business expertise that Tony did not. Part of the secret of Birdhouse's success, they figured, would be to recruit a top-notch team, much like Powell had done with the Bones Brigade more than a decade earlier.

At the end of 1991 Tony left Powell. He and Per would officially launch Birdhouse in January 1992. Although 1991 had been one of the worst years on record for skateboarding, Tony had experienced some measure of success. Besides the contest wins and getting Birdhouse off the ground, Tony won the National Skateboarding Association's championship title—for the 10th year in a row.

New Tricks

Throughout skateboarding's ups and downs, Tony always worked on improving himself, always striving to become a better skater. For the Birdman, improvements meant new tricks. And in the early 1990s there was no shortage of creative board handling from Tony.

Some of his stunts, like the 360 Varial Disaster, were abandoned nearly as quickly as they were named. But certain maneuvers, the Heelflip Varial Lien, for example, inspired Tony with renewed confidence. This trick requires jamming down on the tail of the board to flip it and spin it 180 degrees and then grabbing the board and putting it under your feet.

For Tony, the trick could not have come at a better time. With the rise of the younger vert skaters, Tony felt that his style of skating was becoming outdated. "I was scared of being left in the dust by the new breed," he says. If there was any upside to the downturn in skating in the early 1990s, it was that only the people who truly loved the sport stuck around. In this environment, Tony started Birdhouse and pushed through to what would eventually be his next level of skating.

On the Road Again

Birdhouse Project's beginning was tough. The company could only afford to pay Tony a modest salary, and the money that he had been earning in royalties from other companies was almost gone. There were still many other skate-gear companies—and still very few skaters. Per and

Tony decided that the best way to make Birdhouse known to existing skaters was to go on a demo tour.

They had signed up some of the hottest names to the Birdhouse team, a mix of vert and street skaters including Jeremy Klein, Steve Berra, Mike Frazier, Ocean Howell, and Willy Santos. The team piled into a minivan and spent weeks on the road, sharing beds in motel rooms and eating at Taco Bell. They received little or no money from performing at skate parks around the country.

In all, Birdhouse ended up losing several thousand dollars on this tour. But Tony and the rest of the company thought it was necessary to get people familiar with Birdhouse. At the same time, Tony learned that he was about to become a father: Cindy was expecting their first child.

Little Skater

Hudson Riley Hawk was born on December 6, 1992. Riley, as he quickly became known, demanded a huge lifestyle change during an already strenuous time. Birdhouse was on shaky ground, and Tony thought that with the birth of Riley, now might be the time to consider a new career option.

For as long as he could remember, Tony had been interested in electronics. While he was able to afford it, that hobby continued as Tony collected the latest electronic toys in the mid- and late 1980s. It was something of a natural transition, then, when Tony began to consider video editing as a possible alternative to the skateboarding career that was not going well. Tony had done some work with Stacy Peralta on some of the Bones Brigade videos and discovered that he had an aptitude for editing. With Birdhouse barely hanging on, Tony borrowed some money from his parents to buy some video-editing equipment and launch his new career.

With the money from Frank and Nancy, Tony bought some secondhand editing gear to get his new business venture up and running. Eventually Tony made skating videos for several companies, including Foundation Skateboards and Gullwing Trucks. But he quickly discovered that the money he would be paid for this was substantially less than he needed in order to support his family.

Ultimately, he and Cindy decided that they would have to make some serious changes in their living situation. With the condition of the ramps at Tony's Fallbrook house deteriorating and his skating career completely stalled, the couple put the Fallbrook house up for sale and moved back to Carlsbad. Tony's brief foray into video work was over, and the future was as murky as it had been.

Off the Board Again

Between 1992 and 1993, Tony had skated a total of six contests. Although he fared well in all of them—four first-place finishes and two second-place finishes—the outlook for vert skating was not improving. To make matters worse, the National Skateboarding Association, which Frank Hawk had created in 1983 and had worked so hard to sustain, had completely crumbled by 1992.

Per Welinder and Tony continued to believe that skating was set to make a comeback soon. They continued their low-budget Birdhouse tours, packing skaters into minivans and driving them around the country to skate for practically nothing. But vert skating was not picking up, and Birdhouse was in trouble. In 1994 Tony did not enter a single contest. "Ramp skating was totally dead," he writes in his autobiography. "The checks for prize money would regularly bounce, and usually only 15 skaters would show up to the biggest vert contests."

Tony also had Riley to worry about. Cindy was working too. Between practicing his own skating, running Birdhouse, managing the skate team, and trying to take care of his son, Tony was stretched pretty thin. The situation was not only affecting his business; it was taking its toll on Tony and Cindy's relationship. He and Per met that year and discussed closing down their newfound company. Instead, they came up with another idea. In order to free up some of Tony's time, he would retire from skateboarding—again.

When his Fallbrook house finally sold in 1994, Tony was officially off the board. He still spent some time practicing at the YMCA, but mostly for his own benefit. When he and Frank had to tear down the ramps they had built at Fallbrook, Tony realized an era had come to an end. It was not the only chapter that was closing in Tony's life. That same year, he and Cindy realized that they did not want to stay married. They were both still very much devoted to Riley, but they agreed that it would be best for everyone if they got divorced and shared responsibility for raising him.

Call of the Ramp

Even though Tony had stopped competing, he had not stopped skating. He was still giving demos and practicing as much as he could. In early 1995 the 26-year-old Tony was invited to participate in a show called "Extreme Wheels Live." The weeklong demonstration in Santa Rosa, California, featured skateboarders, Rollerbladers, and BMX bicycle riders. This event, a precursor to the future X Games, was where Tony first met his future wife Erin, who was Rollerblading in the show.

A former competitive ice skater, Erin was participating in the show to pay for her studies at the University of San Diego. Tony and Erin's relationship developed slowly. Tony wanted to make sure that whomever he ended up with would be good with Riley. At first Erin and he were friends, but within a couple months they began dating.

In 1995, for the second time in his career, Tony came out of retirement to help boost sales for his company, Birdhouse Projects. (Associated Press)

Things were looking up for Tony, and not just with his personal life. Business at Birdhouse had started to improve, but it still was not nearly as strong as the company needed it to be.

Tony and his partners made a decision that eventually would send Birdhouse's stake sky-high. They knew they needed to create some recognition for the company. Even though vert skating had not regained its former popularity, they decided to reissue Tony's famous Screaming Chicken Skull board design and get the Birdman back on his board and out into some contests. That was just fine with Tony, who had missed the draw of competition over the previous year. At 26 years old, and for the second time in his career, Tony came out of retirement.

5

EXTREME EXPOSURE

By the mid-1990s skateboarding was coming back. In early 1995, talk of a new Olympic-style competition for television was making its way through the skating community. Rumors abounded as to what the event would be, but it was widely believed that the cable sports channel ESPN would be organizing contests of so-called "action" sports such as skateboarding, Rollerblading, and BMX riding. When the actual plan for the Extreme Games—the original name for the X Games—was finally unveiled, not all skaters were excited about the idea.

Skating for Everyone

Despite its popularity, for more than a quarter-century skateboarding had been a sport of outsiders who had come to like their status. With the start of the X Games many skaters figured that their secret was about to be revealed to everyone. They were right. Ever since the first X Games, skateboarding has become huge. In recent years the number of young skateboarders has multiplied, with millions more flocking to skating than to traditional sports such as baseball. And unlike previous up cycles of skating, after a decade of flying high, fans have not abandoned the sport.

But skaters were not just worried about attracting too many new fans to the sport. They were concerned about how the media would portray them. Newspapers, mainstream magazines, and TV had consistently "gotten it wrong" about skaters—dating at least as far back as the misguided *Life* magazine story in 1965. Hollywood movies had not done much better. Even films in which Tony had participated, *Thrashin'* and *Gleaming the Cube*, for example, portrayed skateboarders as goofballs. For many skaters, skating is more than just a sport—it is a lifestyle. And plenty of them were not sure that they wanted their way of life to be incorrectly magnified for the entire world to see.

There was also the matter of what was being represented at the event. In addition to skateboarding there were contests for activities like bungee jumping, which most skateboarders thought did not belong in such an athletic competition.

Still, the early 1990s had taken such a toll on skating that it was hard to ignore an organized event of this magnitude. For vert skaters like Tony, competitions such as these had just about disappeared by this time. So when the dates for the first X Games were unveiled, Tony's curiosity got the best of him: He headed to Rhode Island, site of the inaugural X Games.

The Extreme Games

The first Extreme Games, held in 1995, marked a major turning point in Tony's career. He finished second place in the street-skating competition and won the vert contest. ESPN took an immediate liking to Tony. He was dubbed the Michael Jordan of skateboarding, and the network showcased him above all other skaters. When the Games were broadcast a few days later, Tony's popularity skyrocketed. He had always been recognized among skaters, but now people on the street knew who Tony Hawk was. Despite the attention he received, at first Tony was not comfortable with the premier skater role that he was thrust into. He was embarrassed at how the network ignored other equally talented skaters when filming, and when he brought it up with ESPN he was told that the network did not have enough time to feature every skater. "Eventually my name and image became synonymous with the X Games," Tony later wrote. "But besides skating the contest, it had nothing to do with me."

The exposure boosted Birdhouse Project's sales too. Suddenly Tony was everywhere. The shoe company Airwalk designed a special Tony Hawk shoe. Tony's income began to edge back up toward what it had been in the late 1980s. He was competing again, and after the X Games he entered the Hard Rock World Championships in Huntington Beach, California, and the Missile Park Monster Mash in San Diego, taking first place in both. All thoughts of a second career in video editing were gone.

A Tough Time

While Tony's career and company were on the rebound in 1995, the Hawk family was faced with sad news when Frank Hawk was diagnosed with terminal cancer. Tony's father had suffered earlier health problems, including two heart attacks, but no one in the family expected the diagnosis Frank was given.

Through the years, Frank had endeared himself to the scores of skateboarders that had passed through the Hawk household. Tony's peers had come to know Frank through his early work with the California Amateur Skateboard League and later when he founded the National Skateboard Association. When news of Frank's illness spread, a steady stream of skaters passed through the Hawk home to wish Frank well.

None, of course, took the news as hard as Tony did. After his victory at the X Games, he returned to Carlsbad to spend time with Frank. Tony was scheduled to leave on a tour for his company, but he had wanted to cancel in order to stay with his father. Frank would not have that. He assured Tony that he would be fine while Tony was on the road. Partway through the tour, while Tony was at Woodward Skatecamp in Pennsylvania, he received an emergency call that Frank had passed away during the night. Tony immediately returned home.

For Tony, Frank's death was not just the loss of one of his parents; it was also the loss of one of his biggest supporters. Frank had been involved in Tony's skating from the beginning. And while Tony may have resented it somewhat when he was a teenager, as he grew older he realized how much Frank had helped him advance his career and his passion.

Still Extreme

By the time the second Extreme Games rolled around in 1996, some of the fears that skaters had initially expressed over such mass exposure were coming true. People who had spent years skating in pools and streets and had dedicated themselves to the sport were suddenly pushed aside by skateboarding's newcomers. The commentators ESPN initially hired did not know much about the sport and frequently made mistakes trying to distinguish one move or style from another. And, perhaps worst of all, they tried to pit skaters against each other.

Tony was also still upset that he had been the focus of so much attention, so in order to make time for other skaters, says Tony, ESPN created a rivalry between him and Andy Macdonald, a rising young skater who had turned pro in 1994. Macdonald was coming on strong in the skating world, and the network figured his and Tony's "matchup" would make for exciting television.

While ESPN was right about Andy's ability—he and Tony would alternate winning the vert gold medals for the next several years—what ESPN and most nonskaters did not understand was that the skaters themselves were not all that interested in competing against one another. Skaters were interested in what they could do themselves on the ramp or on the street. Whenever a skater performed well, the rest of the skaters watching were excited to see a successful, impressive run. And when it was their turn to skate, they just went out and did the best they could. According to Tony, that was something that ESPN and the early X Games announcers did not understand. He said they were "misrepresenting skateboarding on a huge level."

That situation would gradually improve as athletes such as Chris Miller, a skater from the 1970s and '80s, were

Tony signs autographs for fans at a skateboarding clinic in Santa Monica, California. (Associated Press)

brought in to provide commentary. But in the early years of the X Games, there were differences between what was believed to be "interesting television" and what was actually taking place during skate contests. Tony, coming off a triple ankle sprain, took a silver medal in 1996.

Skate Tough

Compared to many other skaters, Tony had been pretty lucky as far as injuries were concerned. Aside from tearing up his knee—a problem that plagues most skaters—a few years earlier, Tony's wounds had been relatively few.

But in 1996, as he was preparing to qualify for the X Games at a competition in California, Tony seriously twisted his ankle. Instead of letting it rest properly, he headed out on a demo tour for Birdhouse.

Since his company's business had increased, the Birdhouse team was now able to travel in an extended full-size van, instead of in the minivans of their first few U.S. tours. It was not until he and the team had actually left for the tour that Tony realized his ankle was not healing. Still, he continued to skate on it.

A couple weeks into the tour, he injured his other ankle. Any doctor would have advised Tony to cut short his travel plans and head home. But since he was in charge of the tour, all of the skaters would have had to cancel if he did. So despite the extreme pain, Tony continued to skate—until he sprained the ankle he had originally hurt a second time. Tony's injuries were so severe that he could not even roll over in his sleep without being woken up from the pain. Luckily he was able to take a month off before the X Games, or he might not have been able to perform at all.

Family Man

Amid his pain, Tony had other things on his mind. His and Erin's relationship had steadily grown more serious. In late 1995 she moved in with Tony. Erin took an immediate liking to Riley. Tony and Erin started to look for a new home that would be big enough for all three of them. When Erin found a house that she liked, Tony decided to surprise her by buying the house—and a ring with which he intended to propose to her. "Big decisions in my life have always come easy and are made without hesitation," says Tony. "It is easier for me to make a life-changing decision than to decide what to get for dessert." Erin accepted the house and the marriage proposal. She and Tony were married on September 28, 1996.

Tony was not only in the market for a new house. He wanted a new skate ramp as well. Since he and Frank had torn down the ramp at Fallbrook, Tony had spent much of his time skating at the local YMCA. But he longed for a place of his own that would give him the freedom the Fallbrook ramp had. Tony discovered a warehouse space in centrally located Irvine, California, that was perfect for him and the rest of the Birdhouse team. And Tony was able to afford a new facility since the X Games had helped boost business. Skating was on the upswing once again.

Bigger than Ever

As quickly as skating had gone underground in 1991, by 1997 its popularity returned to its previous level—and then some. The difference had been the X Games. Skateboarding had been introduced on TV as a legitimate sport. Skaters were now seen as athletes competing on television, being rewarded for riding the board that had so often been dismissed as "a toy."

Leading the charge was Tony Hawk, a clean-cut athlete most parents would be happy to have their child emulate. All of a sudden, a whole new generation of skaters was ready to grab a board and hit the ramp.

With this attention and the third X Games (which had now officially changed its name) right around the corner came increasing demands on Tony's time. Besides practicing, running Birdhouse Projects, and trying to spend time with his family, Tony was overrun with requests for appearances, interviews, and photographs. It quickly became too much for him to deal with. He hired his sister Pat to help manage his exploding career. Tony had thought that having someone organize his schedules and appearances would give him more free time to do the things he needed to do. Instead, his sister and a publicist friend started creating more appearances for Tony. Suddenly, everyone was interested in Tony Hawk and he was everywhere. He had become the most popular skater ever.

For Tony, the days of being labeled a social misfit were past. Even the kids who had made fun of him in school had probably known of his popularity. But with this recognition, part of skateboarding's appeal was lost too. For many skaters, Tony included, much of skating's draw had been its outsider status. Now, being a popular skater meant a life in the spotlight. While Tony did not always care for all this attention, he was more able to adapt to it than many other skaters. "If my role is to be skateboarding's link to the mainstream, I'm willing to accept it," he later told a reporter.

At the 1997 X Games he was able to settle into his role of number-one skateboarder perfectly—according to the skating judges anyway. During his second run on the vert ramp (skaters are given three runs), Tony wowed the crowd and judges with an awesome performance. Those watching the run called it "perfect." Tony did not totally agree with that assessment, but he was very proud of the run. Despite a great performance by silver-medal winner Rune Glifberg, Tony captured the win and the gold. And, in a move that would hint at what was down the road, Tony spent his third run trying to land 900s. "I didn't get close," he says. "At that time, they seemed like a pipe dream."

Big Birdhouse

The company that Tony and Per Welinder had founded was now a success. That summer the Birdhouse team went on tour in style, riding around the country in an RV mobile home. Fans were turning out in huge numbers for their skate demos—it was the good old days all over again.

Tony continued to compete in 1997, winning a vert contest in London and capturing second place at the Hard Rock World Championships in Hollywood. And, as usual, Tony had continued perfecting new tricks throughout the mid-1990s, although at a slower pace than he had previously done. At least one of them, the Frontside Cab Revert, he was able to perform only once, while filming for a Birdhouse Projects ad. "I haven't been able to do it since," Tony says.

The mid-1990s had been an important stretch in Tony's life. Along with happiness in his marriage to Erin, there was tragedy in Frank's death. And on the board Tony's role had changed completely as well. The X Games had taken him into millions of homes and had made him a celebrity. At 29 years old, Tony was nearing the end of his professional skating career—but he had one more really big ride ahead of him.

6

IN THE BIG TIME

Tony wanted Birdhouse Projects to distinguish itself from other companies in the same way that Powell Peralta had stood out years earlier: through video. Many of the smaller gear companies had been producing videos, but although many of them featured good skating, the quality of the production was usually poor. Tony hoped to pick up where *Ban This* had left off and make a high-quality, funny, entertaining video with excellent skating. He planned on turning his Birdhouse team members loose so that they could design their own segments based on their personalities. He even had a name for it: *The End.*

Filming began in early 1998, and Birdhouse set aside $100,000 to shoot his project. The total cost, however, ended up to be nearly twice as much. With sequences by Jeremy Klein, Willy Santos, Bucky Lasek, Steve Berra, and others, *The End* featured explosions, animals, fire, food, simulated injury, and lots of serious skating. It debuted in Santa Ana, California, in October 1998.

But while Tony wanted the video to showcase the personalities of his Birdhouse skaters, he had his own reasons for filming the movie. He wanted to use the film as a chance to realize some of the tricks he had been attempting for years. With the end of his career on the horizon, it was time for Tony to go out the way he had intended. "I wanted the video to be a culmination of my video career," he wrote.

For his segment of the film, Tony had a new ramp designed and specially built that was big enough to accommodate the tricks he planned to include. The 48-foot-wide ramp was more than two stories tall. It was so large that it had to be constructed inside an outdoor arena in Mexico—an arena that usually housed bullfights. Its size frightened even Tony: "I was scared the first time I saw the ramp," he says.

It needed to be as large as it was if Tony was going to be able to successfully execute such stunts as the varial 720 and the 900, tricks that he had not been able to do so far in his career. The ramp also had a 360-degree loop, which Tony intended to skate without falling off. The loop would take Tony in a complete gravity-defying circle—like two half-pipes stacked end on end. He had tried the move earlier in his career for a commercial shoot, but, like the 900, it had proved beyond his ability at the time. But Tony was ready to complete these tricks and move on.

A Short History of the 900

By the time Tony was ready to attempt the 900 for the filming of *The End*, nearly 12 years had passed since he first envisioned the trick. Pulling a 900 had occurred to Tony while he was teaching at a skate camp in France during the summer of 1986. There he had enjoyed plenty of practice time, and it was while he was working on a 540 that he imagined he could add another complete rotation and do a 900. Although he messed around with the move, at that time Tony realized the 900 was beyond his reach.

Ten years passed without Tony seriously attempting the trick again. In that time, skating had bottomed out, and it was just starting to come back. Vert riding was still something that was not practiced by most skaters, who now preferred street skating. Tony had not been skating for audiences as much as he had a few years earlier, so he was excited when he was asked to perform at a demo. When someone from the audience suggested that Tony try a 900, he thought, "Why not?" The result was a bone-crunching drop to the bottom of the ramp.

"It hurts when you fall," says Tony. "Your elbows swell, your knees ache, and your spine crushes into chalk dust from constantly falling 10 feet onto your knees—but remember, skating is fun."

At the same time, a number of other skaters were trying to master the 9 too, including Danny Way, Tas Pappas, Giorgio Zattoni, and Rob "Sluggo" Boyce. Tony, along with these skaters, tried to devise the best method of completing the two-and-a-half turn 900 and landing safely on the board. But as soon as they solved one problem necessary for executing the trick, another would arise: They would lose their boards or they would slam the ramp or they could not stop spinning. "It was like trying to jump out of a washer locked on the spin cycle," says Tony.

He threw himself into studying the problem, and by the end of 1996 he was pretty certain that he would be able to land a 900. Then came the fateful day when, while skating at the ramp owned by gear manufacturer Plan B, Tony completed the 900, only to land on his board and then fall off—hard. He smacked the bottom of the ramp with such force that he broke a rib.

He shelved the trick for a while after that. But during the 1997 X Games, following his "perfect" run in the vert contest, he took another shot at the 900. He was nowhere as close as he had come that day on the Plan B ramp. But by then Tony was determined to do it. He continued to chase the 9 at every contest, and a short while later he made a breakthrough in the spin. Tony was certain his new discovery would help him land the move. Plus, he was preparing to film *The End*.

The new huge ramp would give him the extra room to complete the trick that many of the smaller ramps would not. The high walls on the Mexico ramp allowed Tony to build up amazing speed, which in turn let him gain that much more air as he shot up above the opposite side. Where he could normally gain six feet on airs, on *The End* ramp he could post 10 feet.

Tony was saving his most difficult tricks for the end of the 11-day shoot in case he injured himself. He did not want to lose out on any filming with a cracked back or sprained ankle. Early in the shooting he had successfully completed the varial 720 and the 360-degree loop. All that remained was the 900.

The cameras were rolling as Tony warmed up with a 540. He was ready to go for the 900, when suddenly he was overcome with memories of his bad fall at the Plan B ramp and his broken rib. He tried to forget about that incident, but he was not able to put it out of his head. After abandoning the trick, Tony described it as the worst feeling he had experienced in years. "The unspoken reason for building that ramp had been to land the trick, and I had failed," Tony says.

Despite Tony's failure to land a 900 in *The End*, the film was an immediate and overwhelming success. Tony had managed to cross most of the remaining tricks off his list, and in doing so had helped to produce one of the most popular skating videos of all time. Still, he was mad at himself for not trying to land the elusive trick when he had the chance.

Tony tried to land the 9 a couple more times before the 1999 X Games, but each effort resulted in a painful slam into a ramp. Finally, while competing in the Triple Crown in Asbury Park, New Jersey, in 1998, he tried the 900 for the last unsuccessful time. When he got up off the ramp

Tony has become one of the biggest draws at ESPN's annual X Games. (Landov)

floor, he could hardly stand. Tony's next attempt at the elusive 900 would come during the following summer at the X Games.

The 1999 X Games

By the time the Summer X Games rolled around (there are both summer and winter events), Tony had already made his decision. This was going to be the last year that he competed in skating, not just in the X Games but in all contests. Tony was retiring again, and this time for good. He was 31 years old, and two decades of competition had left him drained. It was not that he was upset or that he did not enjoy skating; he was just tired. And entering contest after contest had begun to feel more like a job than fun, which was the real reason Tony had always wanted to skate.

Plus, Tony was now skateboarding's official spokesman. Other skaters chose him to represent them in dealing with the X Games network, ESPN. He was the most recognizable face the sport had ever seen, which was creating a lot of unexpected circumstances. In 1998, for example, he began to receive endorsement offers from some pretty unusual sources. Tony had long been a spokesman for companies that carried skating-related gear. But now he was being asked to represent products and appear in ads that had nothing to do with skating.

Tony appeared in the "Got Milk?" campaign, a razor-blade spot for Schick, and a commercial for the movie *Tarzan*, among numerous other ads over the years. The offers became so much to deal with that, in addition to his business manager and a publicist, Tony eventually had to hire an agent to help him handle the requests. The pressure was tremendous.

Tony was dealing with other demands as well. In March of 1999, he and Erin's first son, Spencer, was born. Riley was now six years old, and Tony was faced with many responsibilities for his family.

By the time the Summer Games neared, he had made up his mind that he would compete through the end of 1999 and then retire. Before the Games that year, the only competition he had entered was the X Trials in Richmond, Virginia. Tony had not been enthusiastic about competing for more than a year, and as the X Games neared he realized that he was not very excited about them, either. That lack of excitement may have contributed to Tony's less-than-amazing showing on the vert ramp, where he finished in third place for the second year in a row. But looking back on that day, Tony now thinks that finishing in third place might have inspired him to return to his 900 attempts during the Best Trick contest. "It gave me the incentive to go for broke in the Best Trick event," he says.

Tony's skateboarding career has been marked by incredible feats on the board, tricks that would seemingly come out of nowhere and push him light years ahead of other skaters. But no trick has come so unexpectedly, changed so much so fast, or come to be more synonymous with Tony Hawk than the 900 that he successfully completed on June 27, 1999. Not long after landing the 9, one fan asked Tony what was going through his mind as he landed the trick. "It seemed like a giant weight was lifted off my shoulders," he said. "I've been trying it off and on for almost 10 years—and extensively for the last four years."

In an instant, it seems, Tony was the athlete that the entire world had been cheering on for years. Suddenly, skateboarding was the new Great American Sport. "A few years earlier skateboarding had been as passé as you could get," writes Tony in his autobiography, and now fans were battling with security guards just to get Tony's autograph. Tony's trick made news around the world, and, as ESPN began to air his 900 around the clock, congratulations started to pour in from all corners.

Post-900

Tony was tempted to retire after finally nailing the 900 at the 1999 X Games. But he had already decided to finish out that year's contests, and he stuck with that plan. He took third place in the vert contest during a competition in Prague and then headed to the Vans Triple Crown finals in Huntington Beach, California. After capturing first in that meet, Tony decided his career in contests was over. "After hundreds of contests and well over half my life spent competing, I was done," he says. He quietly broke the news of his retirement to a small newspaper.

Finally, Tony was done competing for real. But no matter where he went, people thought that retirement meant Tony was hanging up his board for good. Nonskaters assumed that if he was not competing, he was not riding his board at all. Tony never intended any such thing. In fact, he enjoyed skating as much as ever. He hoped that now that he was free from competing he could return to riding strictly for fun—something that he had not had much of a chance to do in recent years.

7

BEYOND THE BOARD

A funny thing happened when Tony Hawk tried to drop out of competitive skateboarding: He became even more famous. After Tony landed the 900, both he and skateboarding moved into an entirely new realm. Today, nearly 10 years after skating began the climb out of its pit in the early 1990s, Tony is pretty certain that the sport's popularity will not wane again. "The foundation is too solid, too vast," he says. "It may dip down, but I doubt it will dry up."

For the past six years Tony has done his part to ensure that skating remains popular. He has taken his board just about everywhere, from a series of successful video games and instructional skating videos, to TV and movies, and to his traveling road show, the Boom Boom Huck Jam. His continuing ride in the spotlight has kept skaters on their boards and has inspired a new generation of riders. "Tony is the first skateboarder who has given the world a face to

Andy Macdonald (left) and Tony take to the air at the 2000 X Games in San Francisco. (Getty Images)

put on the sport," Tony's friend Stacy Peralta told one reporter. "He has become a part of American pop culture."

But even since his retirement, Tony has retained much of his competitive edge. Although he did bow out of most contests after 1999, he continued entering the X Games vert doubles competition. This event features two skaters on the ramp at the same time in a high-flying, choreographed board ballet. Since 1997, Tony and Andy Macdonald had entered the vert doubles, taking first place in the competition until 2002—six straight years. In August of 2003 Tony collected another gold medal at the ninth X Games in the Best Tricks competition after completing a 900, bringing his total number of X Games awards to 10 gold medals and 16 medals overall. Following the event, Tony said he was finished with skateboard competition for good.

He's Got Game

In addition to his regular appearance on the Boom Boom Huck Jam and other demos, Tony has taken on a new life as a video-game character. And for many young skaters, he is a bigger star on the small screen than he is in real life.

In 1999 games maker Activision released *Tony Hawk's Pro Skater* for the Sony PlayStation. The game went on to become a best-selling title of that year. It was such a hit among skaters and nonskaters alike that Activision quickly began work on *Pro Skater 2,* which was released the following year. By 2004, there were five games in the Tony Hawk series, and another was in development. For Tony, however, *Pro Skater*'s popularity represented more than just an exciting gaming fad. It was a way for young people to get introduced to real-life skateboarding. "There are so many kids who started playing my video game who had never skated in their lives and then they thought it looked cool, so they went out and bought a board and tried it. And they liked it," Tony told an interviewer.

As the 1990s ended and 2000 began, Tony found himself more in demand than ever. Less time spent skating meant more time that he was able to give to other skating-related activities. It seemed that everyone wanted a piece of Tony Hawk's time.

Straight to Videos

In 2000 the Hawk family moved to a larger new home in southern California. A year later, in the summer of 2001, Tony and Erin's second son, Keegan, was born. Riley was nearly eight years old and had already begun skating. Tony signed a contract with ESPN to serve as skating commentator for the X Games, and he also began working on *Tony Hawk's Gigantic Skatepark Tour* for the sports network.

Tony wanted the show to provide a behind-the-scenes glimpse at life on a skate tour. He thought that the image

Tony accepts the ESPN Action Sports Achievement Award, 2001. (Getty Images)

of skating most of the mainstream public had—most of which had come from televised competitions like the X Games—was inaccurate. *Gigantic Skatepark Tour* was being designed by 900 Films, a film company Tony had created. The film project allowed Tony to pursue his long-standing interest in film and video.

While Tony thought that the show would have a decent appeal, he was not prepared for how big of a hit it was. What was supposed to be an eight-episode peek into the skateboarding world turned into a three-season run on ESPN. The shows were broadcast repeatedly, and eventually each season was released as a DVD. Tony found himself in the same situation with the release of another video, *Tony Hawk's Trick Tips*. Originally intended as a basic skateboarding instructional tape, *Trick Tips* proved so popular that Tony ended up filming three volumes between 2000 and 2002.

As Tony's popularity continued to increase, so did skateboarding's appeal overall. Each passing year seemed to find more and more young people picking up boards. Business at Birdhouse was great, and Hawk Clothing and Hawk Shoes, a couple other companies that Tony had started, were both flying high. In 2000 Tony won an ESPY Award, one of the sporting world's highest honors, for Best Alternative Athlete, and the next year he received ESPN's first Action Sports Achievement Award for skateboarding.

Screen Star and Boom Boom Huck Jam

By 2000, Tony was turning up everywhere. Over the next few years he had appearances on several television programs, including *Who Wants to Be a Millionaire*, *Rocket Power*, and *The Simpsons*. He eventually made his way onto the big screen again with smaller parts in *Haggard: The Movie*, Vin Diesel's action hit *XXX*, and an appearance in Stacy Peralta's acclaimed skateboarding documentary *Dogtown and Z-Boys*.

Tony's greatest feat in recent years may be Boom Boom Huck Jam, a high-octane action-sports road show set to music that Tony launched in 2002. Boom Boom Huck Jam, a nonsensical name that Tony and his brother Steve created, features some of the best athletes Tony can assemble, including skaters, BMX and motocross riders, and musical groups whose live songs accompany the action on the ramp.

Boom Boom packs a huge portable ramp that is lugged to different arenas around the United States. The goal, says Tony, is to create a show that can accommodate all the fans that want to attend. During his *Gigantic Skatepark Tour* days, Tony had noticed that fans were being turned away at the door because the parks were not large enough to hold everyone. He would later describe the original idea as a cross between *Gigantic* and the Vans Warped Tour, except that whereas Warped focused on music and skating was sec-

Tony and Erin with sons Spencer (left) and Riley (Getty Images)

ondary, Boom Boom would focus on the skating (and other sports) and the music would be in the background. "The action is the central focus of our show," Tony says.

In its first year the show played 24 cities across the country. The next year it hit 29 towns. And both years Tony was on hand to skate most of the places Huck Jam landed in, even if he did not expect to skate with the tour forever. "The goal is to build something that will live beyond my involvement in it," Tony told one reporter at the outset of Huck Jam.

The Tony Hawk Foundation

In 2001, acting on a $50,000 grant from *Pro Skater* game maker Activision, the Tony Hawk Foundation undertook another of Tony's tasks: building skate parks in needy cities around the country. Tony had established the Tony Hawk Foundation earlier through a personal monetary donation. Despite the explosion in popularity of skateboarding, there are not many places that skaters can engage in their sport legally.

In addition, many of the skate parks built by city departments are not suitable for skaters because of poor designs or transitions, which can result in collision and injuries. This is often the case because the agencies that build these facilities do not consult skaters for their input on constructing usable ramps.

Thus, many skaters prefer the relative ease and safety of skating on streets, sidewalks, and other public places instead. The result, according to Tony's foundation, is that "most serious skateboarders grow up feeling like they're in constant conflict with 'society.'" They may get yelled at, ticketed by police, or run into some other trouble for pursuing the activity they love. So far, the Tony Hawk Foundation has donated thousands of dollars to help create parks from Maine to California, Wyoming to Alaska, and most other states. The goal, says Tony, is to influence the way in which local officials think about skating. Tony wants his foundation to lead by example.

A Late Injury

Tony has had an extremely fortunate life and career. Although two and a half decades of skating have started to take its toll on him, aside from his one knee surgery, Tony had been largely free from injury—until the end of 2003.

Prior to Thanksgiving Tony had been invited to appear on *Wildboyz*, a new MTV show. Tony and Bob Burnquist were scheduled to be filmed with a real-life skateboarding chimpanzee. The two pros were also asked to wear monkey suits while skating Bob's ramp, which included a loop.

During their skate session Tony suggested that they try to skate the loop while in their monkey suits.

Bob made a couple attempts at the loop but bailed on both tries. Still, Tony decided to plow ahead. Later, months after his failed trick, Tony would recount the story on his website. "I dropped in hastily, pumped too hard at the bottom and was leaning too far forward as I started the loop," Tony wrote. "I knew it was bad, so I shot my board out and tried to jump to my feet onto the bottom. But I jumped too far and landed on my hip and eyebrow directly on the flat."

When he regained consciousness, Tony was in an ambulance and the monkey costume, along with his pads, had been cut off of him. As the attendants shifted him from one stretcher to another, Tony felt a severe pain in his side. At the hospital it was revealed that he had fractured the right side of his pelvis, broken a thumb, and sustained a second small fracture above his eye socket, which resulted in 15 stitches through his eyebrow.

After being taken home, Tony was confined to bed for two weeks. He spent the two weeks after that on crutches and nearly another month limping while his pelvis healed. At 35 years old, it was the hardest slam Tony had taken. By January 2004, however, he had recovered almost completely.

Skateboarding's official spokesman (Fashion Wire Daily)

Looking Ahead

Tony has shown no signs of abandoning his passion for skating. That would be difficult to do, given that the sport is more popular than ever. In his autobiography Tony recalls the not-so-distant past when skateboarders were easily recognizable because they were a subculture unto themselves. They "were usually spotted with dark-red scabs, their gait resembled that of a lazy puppet with a tinge of a limp, and they were adorned with baggier clothes than the rest of the population. They were clearly separate from 'normal' people," he writes. Now, says Tony, skaters are everywhere. What was once an underground sport has hit the mainstream. It is one of the fastest-growing activities around.

Despite its popularity, however, there still seems to be a certain segment of the population that does not appreciate skating's appeal, and some groups want to make sure no one else is able to enjoy it either. "I can still walk out my front door, skate to the local school or the curb at the grocery store, and see 'No Skateboarding' signs almost everywhere I look," says Tony. But, he adds, "skateboarding is not a crime—it's my career."

TIME LINE

1968 Born May 12 in San Diego

1977 Brother Steve gives Tony his first board, a blue fiberglass Bahne

1979 Tony enters first contest; wins spot on Oasis park team; skateboarding's popularity begins to diminish as Tony grows more excited about the sport

1980 Sponsored by Dogtown skateboards; father Frank organizes California Amateur Skateboard League

1981 Starts skating for Powell Peralta and sticks with team for next 13 years; skating's popularity plummets

1982 Turns professional; Powell Peralta introduces Tony Hawk signature skateboard with the bird-skull graphic

1983 Frank starts National Skateboard Association; first Bones Brigade video is released; collects first NSA championship award

1985 Tony wins first three NSA contests, the first skater to ever do so; later completes his first 720; shooting begins for second Bones Brigade video, *Future Primitive*

1986 Buys his first house; graduates from high school; cast as an extra in the movie *Thrashin'*; collects six first-place wins; starts work on third Bones Brigade video, *The Search for Animal Chin*

1987 Skating's popularity explodes; Tony retires for first time, but quickly reenters competition; purchases and moves into second house; starts work on fourth Bones Brigade video, *Public Domain*

1988 Finishes in first place in five contests this year; wins another NSA championship

1989 Appears in the film *Gleaming the Cube*

1990 Marries Cindy Dunbar; skating's popularity plummets again

1991 Tony put on "Taco Bell" allowance; places first in seven of nine contests; wins 10th NSA championship; leaves Powell Peralta

1992 Tony's first son, Riley, is born; starts Birdhouse Projects with Per Welinder

1994 Tony retires from skating again to focus on business; he and Cindy divorce

1995 Tony's father, Frank, dies; Tony comes out of retirement; ESPN debuts Extreme Games in Rhode Island, Hawk wins vert competition and takes second place in street; Birdhouse business begins to improve

1996 Marries Erin on September 28; takes second place in the Extreme Games' vert competition

1997 Tony performs one of his best runs ever at the X Games and wins gold; becomes skateboarding's unofficial spokesman; Birdhouse team hits the road in style

1998 Films first Birdhouse video *The End*

1999 Completes the 900 at Summer X Games in San Francisco and retires; best-selling *Tony Hawk Pro Skater* video game created for PlayStation; Tony and Erin's first son, Spencer, is born

2000 Wins ESPY award; *Pro Skater 2* is created; launches *Gigantic Skatepark Tour*; appears on MTV's *Jackass*

2001 Tony and Erin's son Keegan is born; starts Tony Hawk Foundation

2002 Launches Boom Boom Huck Jam

2003 Lands the 900 at X Games Best Trick; retires from competition again; injures self during *Wildboyz* shoot

HOW TO BECOME A PROFESSIONAL ATHLETE

THE JOB

Professional athletes can participate in team sports such as baseball, basketball, and football, or in individual sports such as cycling, tennis, skateboarding, golf, running, or boxing. Professional athletes compete against other athletes or teams to win prizes and money. Here we will focus mainly on becoming a professional athlete in an individual sport.

Depending on the nature of the specific sport, most athletes compete against a field of individuals. The field of competitors can be as small as one (tennis, boxing) or as large as the number of qualified competitors, anywhere from six to 30 (figure skating, golf, cycling). In certain individual events, such as the marathon or triathlon, the field may seem excessively large—often tens of thousands of runners compete in the New York City Marathon—but for the professional runners competing in the race, only a handful of other runners represent real competition.

The athletic performances of those in individual sports are evaluated according to the nature and rules of each specific sport. For example, the winner of a foot race is whoever crosses the finish line first; in tennis the winner is the one who scores the highest in a set number of games; in boxing and figure skating the winners are determined by a panel of judges. Competitions are organized by local, regional, national, and international organizations and associations whose primary functions are to promote the sport and sponsor competitive events. Within a professional sport there are usually different levels of competition based on age, ability, and gender. There are often different designations and events within one sport. Tennis, for example, consists of doubles and singles, while track and field contains many different events, from field events such as the javelin and shot put, to track events such as the 110-meter dash and the two-mile relay race.

Athletes train year-round, on their own or with a coach, friend, parent, or trainer. In addition to stretching and exercising the specific muscles used in any given sport, athletes concentrate on developing excellent eating and sleeping habits that will help them remain in top condition throughout the year. Although certain sports have a particular season, most professional athletes train rigorously all year, varying the type and duration of their workouts to develop strength, cardiovascular ability, flexibility, endurance, speed, and quickness, as well as to focus on technique and control. Often an athlete's training focuses less on the overall game or program that the athlete will execute than on specific areas or details of that game or program. Figure skaters, for example, won't simply keep going through their entire long programs from start to finish but instead will focus on the jumps, turns, and hand movements that refine the program. Similarly, sprinters don't run only the sprint distances they race in during a meet; instead, they vary their workouts to include some distance work, some sprints, a lot of weight training to build strength, and maybe some mental exercises to build control and focus while in the starter's blocks. Tennis players routinely spend hours just practicing their forehand, down-the-line shots.

Athletes often watch videotapes or films of their previous practices or competitions to see where they can improve their performance. They also study what the other competitors are doing in order to prepare strategies for winning.

REQUIREMENTS

High School

A high school diploma will provide you with the basic skills you will need in your long climb to becoming a professional athlete. Business and mathematics classes will teach you how to manage money wisely. Speech classes will help you become a better communicator. Physical education classes will help you build your strength, agility, and competitive spirit. You should, of course, participate in every organized sport that your school offers and that interests you.

Some individual sports such as tennis and gymnastics have professional competitors who are high school students. Teenagers in this situation often have private coaches with whom they practice both before and after going to school, and others are homeschooled as they travel to competitions.

Postsecondary Training

There are no formal education requirements for sports, although certain competitions and training opportunities are only available to those enrolled in four-year colleges and universities. Collegiate-level competitions are where most athletes in this area hone their skills; they may also compete in international or national competitions outside of college, but the chance to train and receive an education isn't one many serious athletes refuse. In fact, outstanding ability in athletics is the way many students pay for their college educations. Given the chances of striking it rich financially, an education (especially a free one) is a wise investment and one fully supported by most professional sports organizations.

Other Requirements

There is so much competition to be among the world's elite athletes in any given sport that talent alone isn't the primary requirement. Diligence, perseverance, hard work, ambition, and courage are all essential qualities to the individual who dreams of making a career as a professional athlete. "If you want to be a pro, there's no halfway. There's no three-quarters way," says Eric Roller, a former professional tennis player who competed primarily on the Florida circuit. Other specific requirements will vary according to the sport. Jockeys, for example, are usually petite men and women.

EXPLORING

If you are interested in pursuing a career in professional sports, you should start participating in that sport as much and as early as possible. With some sports, an individual who is 15 may already be too old to realistically begin pursuing a professional career. By playing the sport and by talking to coaches, trainers, and athletes in the field, you can ascertain whether you like the sport enough to make it a career, determine if you have enough talent, and gain new insight into the field. You can also contact professional organizations and associations for information on how to best prepare for a career in their sport. Sometimes there are specialized training programs available, and the best way to find out is to get in contact with the people whose job it is to promote the sport.

EMPLOYERS

Professional athletes who compete in individual sports are not employed in the same manner as most workers. They do not work for employers, but choose the competitions or tournaments they wish to compete in. For example, a professional runner may choose to enter the Boston Marathon and then travel to Atlanta for the Peachtree Road Race.

STARTING OUT

Professional athletes must meet the requirements established by the organizing bodies of their respective sport. Sometimes this means meeting a physical requirement such as age, height, or weight; sometimes it means fulfilling a number of required stunts, or participating in a certain number of competitions. Professional organizations usually arrange it so that athletes can build up their skills and level of play by participating in lower-level competitions. College sports, as mentioned above, are an excellent way to improve one's skills while pursuing an education.

ADVANCEMENT

Professional athletes advance into the elite numbers of their sport by working and practicing hard, and by winning. Professional athletes usually obtain representation by *sports agents* in the behind-the-scenes deals that determine for which teams they will be playing and what they will be paid. These agents also may be involved with other key decisions involving commercial endorsements, personal income taxes, and financial investments of the athlete's revenues.

A college education can prepare all athletes for the day when their bodies can no longer compete at the top level, whether because of age or an unforeseen injury. Every athlete should be prepared to move into another career, whether related to the world of sports or not.

EARNINGS

The U.S. Department of Labor reports that athletes had median annual earnings of $45,320 in 2002. Ten percent earned less than $14,010, but the highest ten percent make more than $145,600 a year. Some athletes earn considerably more than this.

Salaries, prize monies, and commercial endorsements will vary from sport to sport; a lot depends on the popularity of the sport and its ability to attract spectators, or on the sport's professional organization and its ability to drum up sponsors for competitions and prize money. Still other sports, like boxing, depend on the skill of the fight's promoters to create interest in the fight. An elite professional tennis player who wins Wimbledon, for example, usually earns more than half a million dollars in a matter of several hours. Add to that the incredible sums a Wimbledon champion can make in endorsements and the tennis star can earn more than $1 million a year. This scenario is misleading, however; to begin with, top athletes usually cannot perform at such a level for very long, which is why a good accountant and investment counselor come in handy. Secondly, for every top athlete who earns millions of dollars in a year, there are hundreds of professional athletes who earn less than $40,000. The stakes are incredibly high, the competition fierce.

Perhaps the only caveat to the financial success of an elite athlete is the individual's character or personality. An athlete with a bad temper or prone to unsportsmanlike behavior may still be able to set records or win games, but he or she won't necessarily be able to cash in on commercial endorsements. Advertisers are notoriously fickle about the spokespeople they choose to endorse products;

some athletes have lost million-dollar accounts because of their bad behavior on and off the field of play.

Other options exist for the professional athlete who has reached the end of his or her career. Many go into some area of coaching, sports administration, management, or broadcasting. The professional athlete's unique insight and perspective can be a real asset in careers in these areas. Other athletes have been simultaneously pursuing other interests, some completely unrelated to their sport, such as education, business, social welfare, or the arts. Many continue to stay involved with the sport they have loved since childhood, coaching young children or volunteering with local school teams.

WORK ENVIRONMENT

Athletes compete in many different conditions, according to the setting of the sport (indoors or outdoors) and the rules of the organizing or governing bodies. Track-and-field athletes often compete in hot or rainy conditions, but at any point organizing officials can call off the meet or postpone competition until better weather. Indoor events are less subject to cancellation. However, since it is in the best interests of an organization not to risk the athletes' health, any condition that might adversely affect the outcome of a competition is usually reason enough to cancel or postpone it. An athlete, on the other hand, may withdraw from competition if he or she is injured or ill. Nerves and fear are not good reasons to default on a competition, and part of ascending into the ranks of professional athletes means learning to cope with the anxiety that competition brings. Some athletes actually thrive on the nervous tension.

In order to reach the elite level of any sport, athletes must begin their careers early. Most professional athletes have been working at their sports since they were small children; skiers, figure skaters, and gymnasts, for example, begin skiing, skating, and tumbling as young as age two or three. Athletes have to fit hours of practice time into an already full day, usually several hours before school, and several hours after school. To make the situation more difficult, competitions and facilities for practice are often far from the young athlete's home, which means they either commute to and from practice and competitions with a parent, or they live with a coach or trainer for most of the year. Separation from a child's parents and family is an especially hard and frustrating element of the training program. When a child has demonstrated uncommon excellence in a sport, the family often decides to move to the city in which the sports facility is located, so that the child doesn't have to travel or be separated from a normal family environment.

The expenses of a sport can be overwhelming, as can the time an athlete must devote to practice and travel to and from competitions. In addition to specialized equipment and clothing, the athlete must pay for a coach, travel expenses, competition fees, and, depending on the sport, time at the facility or gym where he or she practices. Tennis, golf, figure skating, and skiing are among the most expensive sports to enter.

Even with the years of hard work, practice, and financial sacrifice that most athletes and their families must endure, there is no guarantee that an athlete will achieve the rarest of the rare in the sports world—financial reward. An athlete needs to truly love the sport at which he or she excels and also have a nearly insatiable ambition and work ethic.

OUTLOOK

Again, the outlook will vary depending on the sport, its popularity, and the number of professional athletes currently competing. On the whole, the outlook for the field of professional sports is healthy, but the number of jobs will not increase dramatically. Some sports, however, may experience a rise in popularity, which will translate into greater opportunities for higher salaries, prize monies, and commercial endorsements.

TO LEARN MORE ABOUT SKATEBOARDING

BOOKS

Badillo, Steve, and Doug Werner. *Skateboarding: Book of Tricks.* Tracks, 2003.

Brooke, Michael. *The Concrete Wave*. Toronto: Warwick Publishing, 1999.

Loizos, Constance. *Extreme Sports: Skateboard!* Washington, D.C.: National Geographic, 2002.

Thatcher, Kevin, ed. *Thrasher Presents How to Build Skateboard Ramps: Halfpipes, Boxes, Bowls, and More.* High Speed Productions, 2001.

Weyland, Jocko. *The Answer Is Never*. New York: Grove Press, 2002.

WEBSITES

Skateboard City

http://www.skateboard-city.com

Bob's Trick Tips

http://www.bobstricktips.com

TO LEARN MORE ABOUT TONY HAWK

BOOKS

Boughn, Michael. *Tony Hawk*. Toronto: Warwick Publishing, 2001.*

Christopher, Matt. *On the Halfpipe with... Tony Hawk*. New York: Little, Brown and Company, 2001.*

Dieterich, Alice. *Tony Hawk and Andy Macdonald: Ride to the Top*. New York: Grosset & Dunlap, 2003.*

Editors of TransWorld Skateboarding. *Tony Hawk: A Life in Skateboarding*. Collector's Issue. Oceanside, Calif.: Time Inc., 2003.

Hawk, Tony. *Hawk: Occupation: Skateboarder*. New York: HarperCollins, 2000.

*Young Adult books

Hawk, Tony. *Between Boardslides and Burnout: My Notes from the Road.* New York: HarperCollins, 2002.

MAGAZINES AND NEWSPAPERS

Gleaves, Rebekah. "Ollie Rides Again," *New Times Broward-Palm Beach* (October 24, 2002).

Layden, Tim. "Making Millions," *Sports Illustrated* 96, no. 24 (June 10, 2002): 90.

Levine, Mark. "The Birdman," *The New Yorker* (July 26, 1999): 68–74.

Mudhar, Raju. "He Was a Sk8erGod," *Toronto Star*, 26 August 2003, sec. C02.

Ruibal, Sal. "Hawk Lands Historic Skateboarding Trick," *USA Today*, 29 June 1999, p. 12.C.

ORGANIZATIONS AND WEBSITES

Ron Buck. "X Games V Leaves Lasting Impression on New Home," former ESPN.go.com network. Available online. URL: http://espn.go.com/xgames/summerx99/gen/news/1999/990703/01336656.html. Downloaded on October 21, 2003.

Dave Finger. "Hawk: In the Nine-Light," EXPN.com. Available online. URL: http://expn.go.com/expn/summerx/2003/story?pageName=030817_skate_bt. Posted on August 17, 2003.

Tony Hawk. "Biography," TonyHawk.com. Available online. URL: http://www.tonyhawk.com/bio.cfm. Downloaded on October 19, 2003.

Tony Hawk. "Road Journal," TonyHawk.com. Available online. URL: http://www.tonyhawk.com/journal.cfm. Downloaded on February 5, 2004.

"Chat Wrap: Hawk Soars to Legendary Status," former ESPN.go.com network. Available online. URL: http://espn.go.com/xgames/summerx99/skate/news/1999/990629/01331161.html. Downloaded on October 21, 2003.

Tony Hawk's website is full of photos, videos, and skateboarding news.

Tony Hawk's Official Website
http://www.tonyhawk.com

The Tony Hawk Foundation supports programs that focus on creating public skate parks.

Tony Hawk Foundation
P.O. Box 1780
El Granada, CA 94018
http://www.tonyhawkfoundation.org

SKATEBOARDING GLOSSARY

backside performing a trick while your body faces away from the ramp

bail to jump out of a trick when you think you will not be able to perform it

demos skating exhibitions usually sponsored by shops or skate parks where pro skaters do not compete against one another, but instead show off their various skills and tricks

fakie a term that means the skater is performing a trick backward

flat the bottom area of a ramp where there is no incline

frontside performing a trick while your body faces the ramp

grab handling the skateboard with your hands while in the air

grind scraping the front, back, or both trucks of a board on a lip, railing, or other surface

half-pipe a U-shaped ramp with high sides used in skateboarding to gain air in order to perform tricks. From the end, it looks like a pipe cut in half lengthwise.

loop a 360-degree structure that requires a skater to ride in a complete circle

ollie a revolutionary trick that consists of popping your skateboard up with your back foot and stabilizing it with your front foot so that you can take yourself and your board into the air

run the time given to a skater to perform his or her event, usually at a contest, as in: "He pulled some awesome tricks during his run."

snake run a twisting, concrete run at a skate park so named for its long, slinky shape

street skating skating performed on natural obstacles such as concrete, railings, and curbs, and that can be done just about anywhere

varial flipping the board in a 360-degree circular rotation without using your hands. This can be combined with many other tricks, as in the Varial 720 or Backside Varial, and was originally named by Eric Grisham after his sponsor, Variflex

vert skating skating performed on a vertical surface such as a half-pipe or ramp

INDEX

Page numbers in *italics* indicate illustrations.

ABOUT THE AUTHOR

Freelance journalist and editor **Todd Peterson** spent several years writing about music and pop culture in northern California before moving to Las Vegas to cover southern Nevada's exciting entertainment scene. Todd moved to New York in 2001, where he continues to write about a variety of topics and edit other writers' work.

When he is not writing or editing, Todd is probably devouring a book or hiding out at the movies. He lives in Brooklyn with his wife and son.